Too Many
BUBBLES

MUCKY PUPS
DÖG
SHAMPOO

EXTRA
BUBBLY

For my Dad, without whom there would have been
no bath and no bubbles, and therefore no book.
And to James Catchpole for giving me a chance,
as well as for his tireless enthusiasm — **DG**

For Bertie the dog, who is sometimes
partial to rolling in nasty things too.
Special thanks to Chloë Forbes at S&S for her
endless positivity during the making of this book — **DT**

SIMON & SCHUSTER
First published in Great Britain in 2020 by Simon & Schuster UK Ltd
1st Floor, 222 Gray's Inn Road, London, WC1X 8HB
Text copyright © 2020 David Gibb • Illustrations copyright © 2020 Dan Taylor
The right of David Gibb and Dan Taylor to be identified as the author and illustrator of this
work has been asserted by them in accordance with the Copyright, Designs and Patents Act, 1988
All rights reserved, including the right of reproduction in whole or in part in any form
A CIP catalogue record for this book is available from the British Library upon request
978-1-4711-8257-0 (PB) • 978-1-4711-8259-4 (EB)
Printed in China
1 3 5 7 9 10 8 6 4 2

Too Many
BUBBLES

David Gibb   Dan Taylor

SIMON & SCHUSTER

London   New York   Sydney   Toronto   New Delhi

Our dog likes nothing better, when we take him for a stroll,
Than finding something **nasty** and going for a roll.

He comes back caked from nose to tail, it's always such a laugh,

Until Mum says it's up to us to give the dog a bath!

So it's **bath time** for the dog!
Let's turn on all the taps.

Shall we add the bubble bath?
A little more, perhaps?

"Now," I tell my brother,
"we should only add a drop."

But once you start to pour it in . . .

. . . it's very hard to stop!

There are **too many bubbles**. They're building up a fog.
It's hard to tell which room we're in, and now we've lost the dog!

There are bubbles on the ceiling
and bubbles round our feet,

Bubbles in the hallway,
and bubbles in the street.

There are **too many bubbles**
and they've reached the market square,

But something's hurtling through the stalls,
as food flies everywhere!

The butcher calls out angrily,

the baker starts to wail,

Whatever's causing all this fuss has left a soapy trail . . .

There are **too many bubbles** and the park is in a mess,

There's something in the fountain
and the ducks are getting stressed.

Its shape is quite familiar,
with a tail, four paws, a nose.

The bubble bath clutched in its mouth . . .
Oh dear! Look there it goes!

There are **too many bubbles** and now they fill the sky,
Swelling ever larger, floating gently by.

They're shimmering. They're beautiful.
They're definitely trouble.

But **where's** the dog?

Oh, there he is – trapped inside a bubble!

There are **too many bubbles** for the animals at the zoo.

The keepers try and catch them but they can't tell who is who!

The dog has got some company.
Look – he's made a friend!

We'd better get them down
before they meet a soapy end.

There are **too many bubbles**,
and my brother's worried sick.

Our dog's in so much trouble now,
we must do something quick.

The police have called the fire brigade, and now the army's here.

There are tanks and soldiers everywhere.

Oh dear, oh dear, oh dear!

There are **too many bubbles** and I'm tired of all this foam.

We just want to find the dog and make our way back home.

But wait, what's that? A rumbling noise?
What could it be? I wonder . . .

Is that a herd of rhinos? No! That's the sound of . . .

There are **no more bubbles**! They've all been washed away.
We're filthy. We're exhausted. It's been a busy day.

The dog's turned up. That's typical. At least **he's** had a laugh.
But now it's time to head back home . . .

...and have another bath!